Prolance

www.prolancewriting.com
California, USA
©2019 The Chronicles of Bani Israil

ISBN: 978-1-7338267-5-4

THE KING, THE QUEEN, AND THE HOOPOE BIRD

By Dr. Osman Umarji
Illustrated by Sama Wareh

PROLANCE

Dedication

To Malik and Ammar.

To Safiyya, whom I began my
adventures in storytelling with.

To Ruqaiya and Ibrahim, for their
support.

To Amina, for her love and
inspiration.

Table of Contents

Prologue

This is a true story. It takes place three thousand years ago. It is about one of the majestic Prophets from the tribe of *Bani Israil*. *Bani Israil* had only recently settled in the land of Sham, a delightfully wonderful place full of beauty, rich with natural resources, creatures of all kinds, and many surprises. However, wherever *Bani Israil* went, mischief was always lurking nearby.

A Father's Legacy

They call me Hud-hud. That means the hoopoe bird. It's pronounced hoo-poo. I have quite the tale to tell you. It's no tall tale, that's for sure. What I am going to tell you is the real deal. It's the truth. I saw it with my own eyes.

It all started years ago, when I would travel alone between the distant lands in the Arabian Peninsula. You may have heard the expression that birds of a feather flock together. That doesn't apply to us. We hoopoes, we don't fly in flocks like most other birds. We don't gather like a murder of crows or a coronation of kingbirds, but we do travel solo or with a mate. In those days, I would fly around, admiring the beautiful valleys, mountains, and deserts. Every time I would fly between the mountains, I would remember the stories I heard about the mountains singing the praises of Allah. I heard this from so many creatures, that no one could dispute it. It was even recorded in a sacred book called the Quran.

Years ago, there was a wise and noble man named Prophet Dawud who would walk these valleys between towering mountains, chanting in Hebrew. His voice was splendid, enchanting, and captivating. When Prophet Dawud recited the beautiful verses from the Zabur, any creature that heard his voice would be so touched that their hearts would be overcome with peace. The Zabur was a majestic book gifted to this prophet of Allah. It was full of beautiful hymns praising Allah and reminded people about the realities and truths of this life. Who gave him such an incredible gift, you might wonder? It was given to him by none other than the One who created me and you. The One who created these mountains and valleys. The One who created the sun and the moon. The One who is the Lord of the entire universe. It was given to him by Allah.

Prophet Dawud would chant the Zabur melodiously. You must believe me when I tell you, he had the most perfect voice any man has ever been given. It was so inviting that the birds who were soaring high in the sky or perched upon the trees

would join him in a magical chorus of recitation.

Ask any ornithologist and they will tell you about the songs that birds can sing. Yellow warblers and mistle thrushes are just a couple of the species of songbirds with amazing vocal skills. In fact, I myself am about the size of a mistle thrush, although we hoopoes are known to be much more beautiful because of our royal crown of feathers, slender beaks, and exotic plumes of tangerine and apricot orange. Now, hearing birds sing is nothing extraordinary. But hearing them chant the Zabur was mesmerizing.

Along with the birds, the mountains would sing and echo the recitation of Prophet Dawud. Every living creature in the valley would rejoice at the ensemble of man, birds, and mountains glorifying Allah. How did the mountains sing? I do not know. The truth is that only Allah knows, for it was a miracle for Prophet Dawud alone.

For as great a king as he was, Prophet Dawud left behind neither money nor wealth. These are temporary worldly possessions that don't last.

Instead, he left behind something far more splendid – good deeds and a lasting legacy. Prophet Dawud's legacy was to leave behind a son. Not just any son, but a son so incredible that he surpassed his own father in wisdom and power.

I was, and forever will be, a humble soldier in the extraordinary kingdom of Prophet Sulaiman, the son of Prophet Dawud. What an honor it was to work for a true servant of Allah. The story I am about to tell shall give you a taste of what it was like to live under the guidance of a prophet.

The King of Palestine

Power is what most kings desire. They aspire to control their subjects and live a lavish life. I know this because I have flown across the east and west and have seen many such kingdoms where the citizens are enslaved to their king and where the rich take taxes from the poor. But the Kingdom of Prophet Sulaiman was different, even with his immense power and wealth. In fact, he had power in ways you could never imagine. How did he get all this power? How did he gain all this wealth? What did he do with such power and wealth?

While most kings are arrogant and believe they are above the law, Prophet Sulaiman was cut from a different fabric. The fabric of prophethood made him humble, and his power was used exclusively in the service of Allah. You see, power often corrupts, but not in the hands of Prophet Sulaiman. He held himself to the highest moral standards.

When I say he had power, I don't mean power in the typical sense. I mean raw, supernatural power that the world had never seen before and will never see again. And believe me, he would need every bit of it to deal with all the problems he would face. It was not magic, although you will hear a lot about magic in this story. The powers that Prophet Sulaiman possessed came from the same source as his father's powers. They were miracles from Allah.

Prophet Sulaiman's rise to power was smooth and natural. He was held in high esteem by his people due to his honorable character and wisdom. He was the son of Dawud, a king and a prophet. He came from noble lineage, so people respected him and everything he represented.

There was no single feature that made him so handsome. He had soft eyes but chiseled cheekbones. He had a few slight wrinkles on his face, projecting wisdom far beyond his age. His shoulders were broad and his chest slightly protruded. His stomach was flat, reflecting the simplicity of his lifestyle and diet. His father used to fast every other day, and Prophet Sulaiman learned there was nothing worse than a man overeating. Food was meant to nourish our bodies, and filling our bodies with excess food was considered dishonorable. He also learned from his father to only eat from what his hands produced, and despite being king, he never relied on anyone other than Allah.

When you looked at his blessed face, you would simultaneously see confidence and humility, as well as contentment and concern.

I never saw it, but it was mentioned that he possessed the seal of Prophethood on his back. All the prophets of Allah had it. The seal was located between his broad, muscular shoulders. It was a raised portion of skin, the size of a pigeon's egg, and had many tiny hairs growing on it.

The Kingdom of Prophet Sulaiman was in the land of Palestine and its surrounding areas. The region was also known as the land of Sham. What a majestic land it was – and still is. Its capital was – and still is – the sacred city of Jerusalem. The entire land of Palestine and the neighboring region was blessed by Allah. How could it not be, when its soil had been trodden upon by so many prophets of Allah? Its land was fertile, with luscious trees and plants growing in the hills and countryside.

Beautiful, dark green cypress trees lined the sides of the roads like a disciplined army standing in ranks. Their wood had a pleasantly spicy scent and was used by carpenters in crafts and other woodwork. Oil was extracted from their leaves and used for its medicinal properties.

Oak trees also grew in abundance. They grew in different shapes and sizes, with striking serrated pear-green leaves. They symbolized longevity, as the trees themselves would live for hundreds of years. They were a source of many blessings for us. Their hard wood was preferred by shipwrights in shipbuilding. The oak flowers were pollinated by the wind and produced copious amounts of tiny acorns that were used by families for baking bread.

Azarole Hawthorn trees were another blessing we enjoyed. They grew at higher elevations and did not grow in abundance. They were significantly smaller than the lovely cypress and majestic oak trees, although they possessed a magnificent inflorescence of white flowers with a greenish-gold center and dark red anthers. They produced tiny azarole fruits in the fall that looked like loquats, but more sour and acidic. We birds loved to stick our beaks into their juicy centers. People would make jam out of them and enjoy it year-round.

There were many other fruit trees in Palestine. However, of all the fruit trees in the land, there were two that held a special place in the hearts of all of Allah's creation: the fig and the olive tree.

Fragrant fig trees grew aplenty and were a source of happiness to birds and humans alike. Standing twenty-five feet tall, they generously produced the sweetest figs every summer for the people and animals of the land. Figs are so unique. Shaped like curvy raindrops, they are inverted flowers with unopened blooms safely protected in their velvety skin. Their flesh comes in bright and dark shades of yellow, orange, and red. They are soft, sticky, and sweet. They have an intense flavor that can only be described as heavenly. By the blessing of Allah, more figs grew than could be eaten.

Despite the birds and beasts sharing a love for figs, it was the blessed olive tree that was the jewel of Jerusalem. The olive trees were exquisite. Their trunks were whimsically gnarled, and beautiful clusters of white flowers grew on their axils. Their leaves were avocado green on top with a silver sheen on the bottom. *Bani Israil* would enjoy olives day and night and export the surplus to the surrounding regions. They would also extract olive oil for cooking and for fuel. The streets would be lit year-round with olive oil lamps.

We birds considered Jerusalem and the surrounding land of Sham as the most precious land on Earth.

There were so many other species of trees that inhabited this blessed land. We would frequent these trees day and night, enjoying their fragrance, fruit, and shade. We would sit perched upon the branches in the early morning, singing while the dew was still on the leaves. We would make our

nests in these trees and wished to spend the rest of our lives here. We weren't the only creations who loved life in Palestine. Humans also revered this land.

Two groups of people lived in the magnificent Kingdom of Prophet Sulaiman: the indigenous Palestinians and *Bani Israil*. Prophet Sulaiman's lineage came from *Bani Israil*, which means the children of Israil. Israil was another name for Prophet Yaqub, who lived several generations before us in Palestine. Prophet Yaqub was the father of Prophet Yusuf. Prophet Musa and Prophet Haroon also came from his lineage. All the descendants of Prophet Yaqub were thus known as *Bani Israil*.

Prophet Yaqub and *Bani Israil* lived in Palestine hundreds of years ago, but they left and resettled in Egypt upon the invitation of Prophet Yusuf. After Prophet Yusuf passed away, *Bani Israil* suffered for generations under the evil Pharaohs in Egypt and wished to return to Palestine. Eventually, they returned after Prophet Dawud led them victoriously into Jerusalem after an epic showdown against the evil Jaloot and his army. But these stories are for another day.

As you can see, *Bani Israil* was blessed throughout history with numerous Prophets from Allah. He favored them time and again, showering them with miracles and blessings. However, their history is rather ignoble. Shockingly, they argued with their prophets and failed to follow their commands. They even had the audacity to fight against and kill their prophets. They often rejected the miracles they witnessed and abandoned the scripture they were commanded to follow. However, they did not dare fight with Prophet Sulaiman openly. They knew he had too much power and was swift in dealing with disobedience.

As for the Palestinians, they had been entrusted with the land since the time of Prophet Yaqub. They cared for the famous fig and olive trees, and they enjoyed all the blessings that Palestine had to offer. They took care of not only the agriculture, but also the illustrious places of worship and historical buildings. However, many of the structures showed signs of wear and tear. The greatest kingdom in the history of mankind could not be left in such shape. Prophet Dawud had begun renovating the city before his death. Prophet Sulaiman took over this responsibility immediately upon his ascension to the throne. He inherited a truly beautiful land, yet there was still much work to be done in his kingdom.

Masjid Al-Aqsa

When Prophet Sulaiman became king of Palestine, one of his first orders of business was to renovate the sacred city of Jerusalem. As capital of the kingdom, Jerusalem had to reflect the religious beauty that the kingdom projected to the world. Prophet Sulaiman held a meeting with his royal council to discuss his vision.

"As humble servants of Allah, we are custodians of this holy city. The symbol of this city is Masjid Al-Aqsa. It is the sacred house of worship built by our forefathers, Prophet Adam, Prophet Ibrahim, and Prophet Yaqub. Believers all over the world turn towards Masjid Al-Aqsa in prayer, and I see that it needs to be renovated and expanded. I consider this to be a great act of devotion to Allah," Prophet Sulaiman proclaimed.

All the councilmembers concurred. "Our Prophet and wise king has spoken the truth. We must dedicate our wealth and energy in seeing Masjid Al-Aqsa expanded and restored," they said.

Immediately, the council gathered the sincere believers from *Bani Israil* and they donated their wealth and time for the masjid. They broke up into teams, with each team working on a specific part of the masjid.

"Listen up," said the foreman as he rounded up the volunteers. "I want your team working on the foundation of the masjid," he called out, as he pointed to a group of the believers.

"Yes, sir. The foundation of the masjid must be built by strong men with strong faith," replied one of the team members.

"And I want a second team responsible for expanding the walls and patching them up," said the foreman.

"Absolutely. We won't leave a single crack exposed," said the leader of the second team.

"Lastly, I need a third team to refurbish the roof and polish it. It should have a lustrous shine," said the foreman. The members of the third team were ready to accomplish this task.

With much physical effort, toil, and

planning, each team worked diligently on their assignments until the project was finally complete.

Prophet Sulaiman was satisfied with the outcome. The foundation was now solid and sturdy. The walls had been expanded and were free of cracks and chips. And the roof looked brand new again, sparkling as the sun's rays shone upon it. He believed he had fulfilled his responsibility towards Masjid Al-Aqsa. He stood at the gate of the masjid and raised his hands in *dua*.

"O Allah. I thank you for allowing me to rebuild this holy place of worship. Please forgive my mistakes and shortcomings. This is an incredible blessing, and in this moment of gratitude I ask you for three things. O Allah, when I make a judgment, make my judgment agree with your judgment. O Allah, grant me a kingdom so great that no one after me will ever possess such a kingdom. O Allah, if anyone leaves their home to pray in this sacred masjid, forgive all their sins so they are as pure as the day they were born. You are indeed the One who bestows all blessings."

I swear by Allah that his first two *dua* were accepted. Prophet Sulaiman's judgments were always wise. His kingdom was indeed like no other kingdom before or after him. As for the third *dua*, its acceptance is unknown to us. It is from the *ghayb*. The *ghayb* refers to the unseen of the heavens and the earth. The *ghayb* refers to the hidden secrets of the universe. The *ghayb* is only known to Allah. No man or creature is privy to the *ghayb*, although there will always be those who claim to have knowledge of it. It is my hope that his third *dua* was accepted, so that every believer who prays in Masjid Al-Aqsa gets a tremendous reward. I heard that one prayer in Masjid-Aqsa is worth 500 prayers. If you get the chance, take a trip there and pray in this grand masjid.

I learned many things from that moment. I learned the power of *dua*. The power of *dua* is spectacular. Allah bestows His favors onto whoever He wills. It is truly remarkable that by raising your hands, or wings, and sincerely asking of Allah, we will be showered by His blessings if He wills it.

Prophet Sulaiman's *duas* were ambitious. He asked for big things. Therefore, learn from his example, and if you ask, ask for the best. No request is too large for Allah to fulfill.

From that moment, I also learned the importance of humility and gratitude. Allah had commanded the family of Dawud to live in gratitude, and Prophet Sulaiman was the master of *shukr*. Our Prophet did not show the least bit of arrogance, despite accomplishing as monumental a task as rebuilding Masjid Al-Aqsa. Instead, he attributed all power and success to Allah, and he thanked Allah for allowing him to participate in such a noble act. It was small acts like these that made him such a big man. If mountains are built out of innumerous tiny pebbles, righteous people are made from an abundance of good deeds, even if they are small. Never forget that, my friend.

Miraculous Superpowers

Now I must inform you how Allah responded to Prophet Sulaiman's *dua* for a kingdom so
powerful that no one after him would ever have
such a kingdom. However, you must first understand why Prophet Sulaiman wanted such power in
the first place.

Prophet Sulaiman observed his father rule
for many years. Throughout his life, Prophet Dawud
imparted wisdom and transmitted prophetic values to Sulaiman and his other children. Amongst
the core values he learned were the importance of
righteous leadership, justice, and the obligation to
spread the message of Allah.

Young Sulaiman grew up listening to stories
about *Bani Israil* and how they were mistreated by
the Pharaohs of Egypt. He heard about the torture
and punishment inflicted on *Bani Israil*. Troubled
by this kind of oppression, Prophet Sulaiman became obsessed with establishing justice. He saw
firsthand how a righteous ruler, like his father,

could bring peace and justice to the land. All of these stories and experiences made Prophet Sulaiman yearn for the power to ensure that justice was served and that the word of Allah was spread throughout the land. He realized that having a powerful kingdom would give him the opportunity to enact those values that were so dear to him.

Allah gave Prophet Sulaiman the powerful kingdom that he sought. You must be wondering how. Everything is simple to Allah. He only has to say "be" and it becomes. This included Allah granting his prophets powers that defied the human mind and the physical laws of the universe.

Allah gave Prophet Sulaiman many superpowers. The superpowers were real. These superpowers were miracles from Allah. All Prophets were given miracles as proofs of their prophethood. Many people throughout history claimed prophethood, but when they failed to prove it with miracles, they were exposed as liars. Thus, the miraculous superpowers of prophets convinced the people that they were guided by Allah, and the miracles were a source of comfort to their hearts.

The first miracle given to Prophet Sulaiman was the power to control the wind, especially the wind of Palestine. By waving his hand and invoking Allah by saying "*bismillah*," the wind would blow as fiercely or gently as he willed. Wind could be used in the most wonderful ways imaginable. It could be used as a blessing to provide a cool breeze to the people of Palestine or pollinate the trees in the surrounding area. He could also use the wind to wreak havoc and devastate opposing armies during battle. The opportunities for using the wind to his advantage were limitless.

Not only could Prophet Sulaiman command the direction of the wind to do his bidding, he could also control its speed in fantastic ways. With the morning wind blowing behind its sails, a ship full of goods or soldiers could travel the distance of what would normally take a month in just half a day and return with the afternoon wind by sunset. This was just one of his many miracles, and the people were in absolute awe and amazement of it.

The next superpower that Allah gave him was vital to the development of his kingdom. Prophet Sulaiman was given the power to control a spring of liquid copper that provided him with an infinite supply of metal. The spring gushed forth from the ground with shiny, red copper. Copper melts at nearly 2,000 degrees Fahrenheit, so to see a spring flow with liquid copper without any human intervention was incredible. It was truly one of the wonders of the world.

From this copper spring, Prophet Sulaiman would create various metal alloys such as bronze and brass for the diverse needs of his kingdom. Enormous statues, gigantic bowls the size of water reservoirs, and firmly anchored cauldrons were all built from these metals. If you are wondering how such colossal objects could be built, know that Prophet Sulaiman never had to use his own hands or rely on the limited strength of human beings. Rather, it was another superpower of his that enabled all his orders to be manifested. This superpower was the most intriguing of all. However,

before I can explain this superpower, you need to
know about the intriguing creatures that lived in his
kingdom.

The Jinn

Living amongst the inhabitants of Palestine, as well as throughout the rest of the world, were the *jinn*. The *jinn* are creatures made from smoke-less fire that are invisible to the human eye. No one truly knows the physical reality of *jinn*, not even us birds. So we can only speculate about their nature. It is possible they live in a different dimension than humans and animals altogether. Or perhaps they exist as energy and are transported from place to place by electromagnetic waves. This would explain why humans can't see them, as humans cannot see all spectrums of light. While ordinary fire possesses an extremely weak magnetic field, could it be that the special smokeless fire that *jinn* are made of possesses an incredibly strong magnetic field that allows them to travel as electromagnetic waves at the speed of light? The speed of light is 186,282 miles per second! This is all speculation on my part. Only Allah knows the truth. What we do know for sure is that *jinn* can travel incredibly fast.

The *jinn* are intelligent beings with free will. That means they can make choices about what to believe in and what to do. There are *jinn* who believe in Allah and *jinn* who disbelieve in Allah. There are *jinn* who do good and *jinn* who do evil. There are *jinn* who accepted Sulaiman as a prophet and *jinn* who rejected him. Why am I telling you all this about the *jinn*? I am telling you because the evil *jinn* created a lot of problems for Prophet Sulaiman due to their surreptitious and sneaky behavior. They were a thorn in the side of Prophet Sulaiman's kingdom that he would have to deal with for many years.

Are you are wondering what the *jinn* used to do? Let me take a step back and tell you about their shenanigans and the origins of their mischief.

Babylon

The kingdom of Babylon was one of the most ancient civilizations of Mesopotamia. It was famous for its history and huge population. Babylon was five hundred miles from Jerusalem, and the kingdom was built right on the Euphrates river. What did the people of Babylon believe in? Strange things. Very strange things. The Babylonians believed in a religion that was a concoction of astrology, sorcery, and magic.

They believed that there were seven gods represented in the sun, the moon, and five other planets. As for astrology, they believed that the position of celestial phenomena and weather patterns were omens of things to come in their kingdom. For example, if the sighting of a new moon in the cloudy sky coincided with a victory in battle, future moon sightings in cloudy weather were believed to be good omens. If a lunar eclipse occurred before a defeat, then future lunar eclipses would be considered bad omens. They wrote these omens down on numerous tablets that were then studied through-out the land.

Do these people not think? How absurd to believe in such nonsense. Prophet Sulaiman taught us that the heavenly bodies, such as the sun, the moon, and all the planets, have been placed in an orbit by Allah and they move in a fixed pattern. Yet the absurdity of the Babylonians did not stop at such ridiculous beliefs about astrology.

They believed in all sorts of sorcery and magic. I am not talking about silly magic tricks where a man pulls a rabbit out of a hat or a coin from behind your ear. I am talking about a serious belief that magic could change the fortune of peo-ple. It involved *jinn* and sorcerers working together in Babylon to beguile its people with trickery. The *jinn* would climb on top of one another from the earth to the lowest level of heaven and eavesdrop on the conversations that the angels were having. If they happened to hear about an upcoming event, such as the upcoming birth or death of a person, they would quickly pass the information from one another until one of the *jinn* told a sorcerer. The sorcerer would then tell the people about this one event and mix in a hundred other lies. Many people became easily deceived and began to believe the sorcerers and *jinn* had supernatural powers.

The *jinn* could also travel and communicate with incredible speed. A *jinn* might see a solar eclipse in one country and then rush within a second to another country and tell its people that it knows the future and that a solar eclipse will occur later today. When the people would see the eclipse in fact occur, just as the *jinn* told them, they began to believe that the *jinn* knew the *ghayb*. Very soon, rumors began to spread throughout Babylon about the mysterious power of the sorcerers and *jinn*. However, they had no real power. All power belongs to Allah. He grants it to whomever He desires, and He did not grant any such power to the *jinn*.

The ultimate goal of these devil *jinn* was to get people to disbelieve in Allah and to destroy families. They would use all forms of deception to make a husband and wife turn against each other.

I'll tell you one of the most tragic stories I heard about family destruction. It began when a lady visited a sorcerer.

"Dear powerful sorcerer," she said. "I come to you today seeking knowledge of the *ghayb* that you have."

"My dear lady, I will tell you something from the *ghayb* that I know about your husband," the sorcerer replied, further ensnaring the lady.

"Yes, O powerful sorcerer, please tell me what you know," she said.

"Your husband does not love you anymore. He wishes to marry someone else. I can make him love you forever, but you have to listen to me," said the sorcerer.

"I will do anything you say," the lady replied, horrified by this news and ready to do whatever it took to win her husband back.

"You need to bring me three hairs from your husband's beard. I will need these to cast a spell on him that will make him love you forever," the sorcerer explained. "When he falls asleep tonight, take a blade and cut off three hairs and bring them to me tomorrow."

"I will. Thank you for your help," said the lady.

True to his wily ways, the sorcerer then went looking for the lady's husband and spoke to him to further stir up mischief.

"My dear sir," said the sorcerer. "I want to tell you something from the *ghayb* that I know about your wife."

"Yes, please tell me. What about her?" the husband asked.

"Your wife is planning to kill you. She will come to you while you are asleep with a blade and try to slit your neck. Do not fall asleep tonight, and be cautious of her," the sorcerer warned.

"Thank you for the advice. I will be vigilant," said the husband, shaken by the idea that his wife was plotting to kill him.

Later in the evening, the man laid down in his bed. He snored loudly as he pretended to be asleep. Once his wife thought he was asleep, she came to him with a blade to cut off three hairs of his beard, just as the sorcerer had asked of her. As she neared her husband's beard with the blade poised, the man opened his eyes and grabbed the blade from her. Then, in one swift movement, he stabbed her with the knife and killed her.

Just like that, a sorcerer could destroy a family. My advice to you is to never listen to a fortune teller or sorcerer. They are the worst of liars. They know nothing, but they use their wiles to trick and deceive people into believing untruths and falsehoods. However, they are not the only evil doers. Let me tell you about another group of people who caused us just as much trouble.

There was a group of people from *Bani Israil* who abandoned the guidance of the Torah. They had become enchanted by the religion of Babylon and threw their scripture aside in favor of sorcery and "magic." They dedicated themselves to the *jinn* and the sorcerers and rebelled against Prophet Sulaiman. These misguided people would secretly tell others that it was the *jinn* who had real knowledge of the world, rather than Prophet Sulaiman. They spread rumors that the *jinn* knew the *ghayb*. This was what Prophet Sulaiman had to deal with. How could he go up against an invisible creature that was incredibly sneaky, fast, and strong? But everything is easy for Allah. He gave Sulaiman an incredible superpower to deal with the *jinn*.

Shackles and Servitude

Another miracle that Sulaiman was given was the superpower to control the disbelieving *jinn*. He had the power to capture them and put them in shackles. He enslaved them and made them do hard labor for the kingdom.

One group of *jinn* was ordered to do manual labor. They built many of the structures in the kingdom. They constructed buildings and colossal statues of lions and other beasts that were placed throughout the kingdom. Now I must tell you yet another special trait of Prophet Sulaiman – building statues was permissible under his rule, although it was prohibited under the laws of many other prophets. These *jinn* also built gargantuan bowls and cauldrons that were more than a hundred feet wide and a dozen feet deep.

Another group of *jinn* had a very different task. They were deep sea divers who would go into the ocean to mine precious metals, gems, and pearl oysters. They would also gather gold, silver,

diamonds, and other minerals. These *jinn* would
dive thousands of meters deep to get to the ocean
floor. You must be wondering, how could they do
this? I don't have the slightest idea. Unlike humans,
the *jinn* can breathe underwater. Like I told you
before, the *jinn* are creatures from the *ghayb* that
we don't know much about. All I know is they could
get from Jerusalem to the shore, dive into the sea,
and return quickly with vast amounts of precious
jewels and metals. Just imagine how much wealth
and natural resources Prophet Sulaiman gathered
this way! Perhaps now you can appreciate how he
amassed so much wealth and became the most
powerful king in the world.

Yet another group of *jinn* became soldiers in
Prophet Sulaiman's army. These *jinn* were incredibly
strong compared to other *jinn*. Being strong, fast,
and invisible made the *jinn* valuable in our military operations. I will tell you more about our army
soon.

The superpowers that Prophet Sulaiman
possessed were so fantastic that evil rumors began

to spread that he was practicing magic. These rumors caused much confusion in the kingdom. Some folks ignorantly wondered if Prophet Sulaiman was merely a magician or a sorcerer. However, these lies would soon be exposed. *SubhanAllah*! Prophets do not resort to witchcraft, sorcery, or any form of magic. Rather, all his powers were miracles from Allah that defied the natural laws of the universe known to man.

But not everything about Prophet Sulaiman was miraculous. While he was incredible in so many ways, in some ways he was like any other human. Humans love animals. They marvel at the sight of a tall, majestic giraffe and are mesmerized by the sight of an imposing elephant. But they don't love only large beasts. They also love to watch birds and listen to them sing, especially to a handsome hoopoe like myself. However, there is one animal that stands out from others that Prophet Sulaiman loved the most. Let me tell you something about his relationship with that special creature. It will help you understand the purity of his heart and gentleness of his soul.

Equine Love

Prophet Sulaiman was a busy man. Between administering the affairs of his kingdom and inviting people to believe in Allah, he had very little free time. One of the fascinating things about our Prophet was that anytime you looked at him, you would find him in a state of *dhikr*. *Dhikr* means remembering Allah. He would either be reciting the Zabur or Torah, making *istighfar* (seeking Allah's forgiveness) and *dua*, or thanking Allah. In the very few moments he had some free time, however, you would find him in the stables of Jerusalem.

Prophet Sulaiman loved horses. Not only were his horses loyal soldiers in battle, but they were a source of peace and comfort for him. Allah had blessed him with horses of the highest breed. They were graceful and had the most beautiful manes and coats. They were extremely fast, gloriously galloping when commanded. Prophet Sulaiman had many trainers and handlers who cared for his horses.

One afternoon, he was invited to attend a special exhibition of his horses. The horses came out from behind a large curtain, displaying their beautiful coats of various colors. Some were chestnut colored with white stockings. Others were pure white. They began demonstrating different gaits, including the trot and canter. They showed their gracefulness with every step. Next, they performed a series of dressage movements, including airs above the ground. In these elaborate movements, the horses would stand on their hind legs in different ways. In one move, the horses would lift their forelegs in the air and tuck them back towards their body, distributing all the weight on their hindquarters. This move demonstrated their superb balance. In another move, they would lift their forelegs and jump off their hindquarters, followed by landing perfectly on all four legs.

These moves were important in training the horses for battle. Horses had to be physically capable of jumping in cases where the army had to cross over moats or other obstacles. Only the most powerful and well-trained horses could perform these moves.

Prophet Sulaiman was thoroughly enjoying the exhibition and expressed his appreciation.

"Indeed, I was made to love horses by Allah," he said. "The Torah praises horses for their courage. Horses are from the finer enjoyments of this life. *Alhamdulillah*, Allah has blessed me with the best horses in the world."

As the horses completed their exhibition, they were led by their trainers behind the curtain.

Sulaiman expressed his desire to see them again. "Bring them back to me," he ordered.

As the horses were brought back, he gently stroked their necks and legs and continued to thank Allah for this blessing. Prophet Sulaiman appreciated them immensely. His horses were an important part of his army of fearless fighters. They would rush towards the enemy with passion and courage. For this loyalty, they had earned his love. His horses were special, as was his entire cavalry. Now, I finally get to share the story of our army with you.

An Enchanted Army

Amongst the miracles of his extraordinary kingdom was the formation of an indomitable army. I am proud to say I quickly became an important soldier in the army. It is natural to wonder how a tiny bird with an erratic flight pattern and irregular wing beats could rise up the ranks of the most powerful army known to the worlds. I am a humble bird, but I know my strengths. I am not as graceful as a swan or as exotic as the birds of paradise. However, I can fly extremely high to avoid predators and Allah blessed me with incredible eyesight. I can see water from high above and inform the army. These skills were valued by our prophet and king, as he sought soldiers with unique skills.

Prophet Sulaiman's army consisted of strong men in armor, lightning fast creatures made from smokeless fire, birds that flew high above, and many animals. The army was highly disciplined. Every soldier knew that the slightest act of insubordination would be met with swift consequences.

Prophet Sulaiman was strict, yet his justice made him beloved to all reasonable humans and animals.

Having a highly skilled army was fundamentally important to the kingdom. In fact, the army had a history of fighting battles against oppressive nations dating back to the time of Prophet Dawud. We never fought an unjust battle. Rather, our job was to protect all the inhabitants of the land. To accomplish this, we would march regularly, patrolling the region for any problems to resolve. Every creature had its role to play.

The humans were responsible for patrolling the ground. Each rank of soldiers played a specific function in Prophet Sulaiman's army, and they were trained in the art of various weaponry. Some foot soldiers were experts in archery. Other men were skilled in hand-to-hand combat with swords.

Fortunately, the men in Prophet Sulaiman's army possessed the finest armor known to mankind. Just a few decades ago, Prophet Dawud had solved the centuries-old problem of how to engineer proper body armor. During his time, soldiers

wore extremely heavy metal plates as armor to protect themselves from arrows, spears, and swords.
Unfortunately, the immense weight slowed them
down and wearing a large rectangular plate of steel
made it incredibly difficult for soldiers to maneuver.
One day, Prophet Dawud was holding iron ore in
his hands, thinking about how to better craft armor
for his soldiers. Suddenly, the iron began to mirac-
ulously melt in his hands and became as soft as clay.
Allah had given him the miraculous ability to mold
iron with his bare hands. He was inspired by Allah
to design precisely sized metal rings and link them
together to form chain mail, which is a full mesh
shirt made of these metal links. This form of armor
was significantly lighter, making the soldiers more
agile than ever before. Prophet Dawud and the soldiers were quite grateful for such an invention.

Now the *jinn* had a very different role.
Since the *jinn* could move so quickly without being seen by humans, they would be used for covert
operations such as gathering intelligence about an
enemy. They could also retrieve things for Prophet

Sulaiman from far away with lightning speed in just a few moments.

We birds were very important to the army as well. I myself had some skills that came in handy. My first responsibility was to be on the lookout for water for the army to drink from. Marching across the land for many miles, whether it be a dry desert or green pastures, required a lot of water to quench the thirst of thousands of soldiers. With my acute eyesight, I could spot rivers, lakes, streams, and even groundwater from high above and inform Prophet Sulaiman which way to march. Thus, I became beloved to our Prophet and was in his good grace for quite some time.

The rest of the birds had various responsibilities. Some species had an incredible sense of navigation, with the ability to fly back thousands of miles from home using the fastest route. These birds served as the "GPS" (global positioning system) of the army. They would inform the army of the best routes to take to and from an expedition. Other species would form impressive murmurations comprising tens of thousands of birds, soaring through the air in unison like flying magnets. They could strike fear into the hearts of the enemy and demonstrate the discipline of the army. Finally, the most trustworthy birds were spies, flying clandestine missions to report on the affairs of other civilizations. I was fortunate, *Alhamdulillah*, to be one of these special feathered soldiers of Prophet Sulaiman.

I have done my best to tell you about the great army we had. But you must be wondering how Prophet Sulaiman could communicate with the birds, the *jinn*, and other animals. Be patient, and I will tell you in good time.

Spy Mission

One bright and sunny day I was out on an adventure, flying through the warm sky in search of any important information I could relay to Prophet Sulaiman. I did this often, as one of my jobs was to keep an eye out and report anything that would interest our great leader. He was very keen to get reports from us on what was happening in other nearby lands. Most times I would just go out and return quickly, with nothing to report, since usually nothing interesting would happen. Prophet Sulaiman also demanded punctuality, so all his soldiers reported back on time to avoid his anger. However, on this fateful day, I would not make it back on time, and my life would be changed forever.

I was soaring above the Kingdom of Saba, which was located in the southern part of the Arabian Peninsula. It was a beautiful and fertile land, with vegetation all around. I could see an enormous dam that channeled water around the entire region and irrigated two incredibly lush gardens. One garden was on the left of the kingdom and one was on the right. I could smell the fragrant flowers, fruits, and vegetables even from high above.

It seemed like a normal day, and I did not immediately notice anything out of the ordinary. But then something caught my eye. Thousands of people were gathered below. What was going on?

I descended to get a better look. The people were surrounding a woman who was sitting on a magnificent throne. This was quite peculiar to me, since I was only used to seeing our majestic Prophet Sulaiman standing before his people in such a fashion. I thought to myself, "Who is this woman? Is she a princess? Is she a celebrity?"

Never in my wildest dreams would I have guessed that this woman was the leader of her people. I had never seen a woman leading her people in all my flights over countless tribes, villages, and civilizations. This woman was the royal Queen of Saba, Queen Bilqis. There was no king who ruled the people. Rather, Queen Bilqis was the sole leader of her people. I flew down as fast as I could and

spied a beautiful tree from where I watched her descend her throne and address her people. They stood before her and quietly listened to her speech.

"Your god is so bright and enormous that he provides warmth to the entire world," she began. "Your god is so powerful that his rays nourish the trees and plants. Your god is so large that all the planets rotate around him. Thank your god and worship him with all your heart."

After she concluded her speech, all the people, including Queen Bilqis, began to engage in a very strange form of worship. I must explain this to you.

This strange ritual reminded me of other absurd types of worship that I had heard about before. I heard about people who worshipped their king, like the ancient Egyptians who worshipped the Pharaoh. I had also heard about people who worshipped the stars during the time of Prophet Ibrahim. However, what I was seeing with my own two eyes was something I could never fathom in a million years. The people were all engaged in a ritual of sun worship. They dropped their knees to the ground and prostrated to the sun. They chanted in unison, praising the sun with all kinds of expressions. They were deeply involved in this ritual and fully devoted to the sun as their god. I was flabbergasted and speechless.

How could people believe that the sun was god? How could people believe the sun had any power itself? Did they not know about Allah? As soon as the ritual was completed, Queen Bilqis ascended her throne and was carried towards her palace. I darted from the tree, flapping my little wings as fast as I could to inform Prophet Sulaiman of what I had seen. I knew he would be astonished by this news. However, the army had already left for a training expedition, and it would take me a while to reach them from the south of the Arabian Peninsula, where Saba was located. I had to hurry.

The Power of Language

While I was on my way back from the Kingdom of Saba, some very interesting things happened to the army. Another bird informed me about these events, since I was not there to witness this firsthand. Unfortunately, I would miss out on many remarkable events because I was traveling so often for Prophet Sulaiman.

Prophet Sulaiman stood before the inhabitants of his kingdom. He had gathered everyone to witness the spectacular army and bid them farewell as they marched forth on a long journey. Being the perfectionist that he was, he inspected each soldier carefully. That should not surprise you, as all Prophets practiced and taught *ihsan*, the ancient art of seeking perfection.

To practice *ihsan* means to always act with integrity and diligence because you know that Allah is watching you. Prophet Sulaiman had learned from his father, Prophet Dawud, to practice *ihsan* and gratitude in every action, big or small. Thus, he ensured each soldier was in their proper place in line, standing appropriately with their back straight. He stepped back for a moment as he gathered himself to give a speech to his citizens. His gaze turned left, then right, and he felt a deep sense of gratitude wash over him when he saw his masterfully disciplined army before him. The men were on one side, the *jinn* on the other, and the birds were organized above them in the sky. The birds had their wings spread out, gracefully soaring and providing shade to Prophet Sulaiman and the army with their majestic wings.

At that moment, when the birds' wings were spread open, many of those present experienced a flashback to a very sad day – the day of Prophet Dawud's death. On the sorrowful Saturday that he passed away, the sun was burning hot, scorching the ground and beating on the blessed body of Prophet Dawud and the thousands of people who were attending his *janaza* prayer. The *janaza* prayer is a funeral prayer where we ask Allah to shower His mercy and forgiveness on the deceased. Prophet

Sulaiman stood there, solemnly praying for his father in the sweltering heat, but he did not like the way the sun was beating on his father's body. Prophet Sulaiman's beautiful, blessed eyes turned towards the sky at the condors, eagles, and other large birds above him. He commanded them to provide shade to Prophet Dawud and they followed his command immediately. In fact, so many birds spread their large wings across the sky that the entire ground below was shaded. What a sight to look up and see hundreds and thousands of wings spread out in the sky, completely blocking out the heat of the sun.

As Prophet Sulaiman cleared his throat, everyone returned to the present moment. He turned towards the people. "*Alhamdulillah*. All praise belongs to Allah, the One who has favored us over so many of His believing servants. Oh people, Allah has allowed me to inherit wisdom, power, and prophethood from my noble father. We have been given many miracles and superpowers. My people, know that we have been taught the language of the birds and other animals. Verily, we have been given everything one could imagine. Look at my kingdom around you. No man in the history of the world has ever been given such a kingdom. This is all an incredible blessing. All praise and thanks belong to Allah. *Alhamdulillah*."

There was pin drop silence whenever the Prophet spoke. The strength of his voice and the wisdom in his words captivated his audience. They were attentive and focused on every word. What they heard was nothing new, for they were aware of the infinite blessings that Allah had bestowed upon His great prophet. However, it was the habit of Prophet Sulaiman to remind himself and others of Allah's blessings.

The people and *jinn* wondered how Prophet Sulaiman could communicate with the birds. How could he understand them? How could he speak to them in their language? I have no answer for you. There are some secrets that Allah does not reveal to His creation. There was no one before and no one after Prophet Sulaiman who had mastered the languages of the birds. In fact, I should clarify, Prophet Sulaiman not only knew the languages of birds, but the languages of all animals, big and small.

The army marched forward. Step by step, in perfect unison, each soldier kept his place in the ranks. The soldiers marched for miles, over various landforms, from mountains to valleys. The birds above were also in perfect order, maintaining their position in the army's formation as they flew majestically over the foot soldiers. The army moved forward mile after mile, until it finally reached a beautiful valley in central Arabia. The indentation of this particular valley was the perfect spot for a colony of ants to live in. This ant colony must have had hundreds of millions of ants, but only Allah knows their exact number. Although Allah was aware of the ants, Prophet Sulaiman's army was oblivious to the ant colony living in this valley.

Pay attention to what I am about to tell you, for this part of the story is so astounding that my feathers tingle every time I tell it. As they marched between the scenic mountains, the soldiers at the front of the army did not dare look up or down. They were completely focused and looking straight ahead, as they had been commanded. Only the birds were fortunate enough to be able to enjoy the beauty of the landscape around us. One stunningly beautiful mountain to the left, another chiseled mountain on the right, and a gorgeous valley in between that was flat and a little dry. One of the ants noticed the imposing soldiers as they got closer to the colony. She could hear their heavy boots pounding on the earth with every step, "click-clack, click-clack, click-clack." She realized that if the soldiers continued walking towards the colony, countless ants would be crushed to death. She thought quickly, turned towards the colony, and said, "O ants! Enter your nests immediately and hide so that you do not get crushed by Sulaiman and his army. They are not aware of us!" Within milliseconds, the entire colony rushed back into the holes that they had burrowed into the ground.

You must be wondering how the ant could speak. Well, you might be surprised to know that it was not communicating like people or birds do with audible sound. Rather, ants use pheromones to communicate. Pheromones are chemicals that an ant releases from its antennae into the air that other ants can smell and taste. This is their form of communication. In fact, ants are known to release special alarm pheromones when something distracts them from their work. It may have been that this ant heard the footsteps of the soldiers and released this emergency message to all the members of the colony.

Shortly after the ants ran back into their nests, Prophet Sulaiman called out, "O soldiers! Halt immediately." The entire army obeyed the order of the Prophet and didn't take another step. Prophet Sulaiman walked slowly near the ant colony and gazed upon the dark black ants below. The corners of his blessed mouth turned upwards, slightly revealing his perfect teeth. The muscles on his chiseled cheeks flexed, and his eyes twinkled. He flashed the most radiant smile and laughed out of the immense joy, happiness, and satisfaction he

felt upon hearing the speech of the ant. He raised his muscular hands out in front of him as he would often do when making *dua* and in a loud voice said:

"My Lord, grant me the ability to show gratitude for the blessings which You have bestowed upon me and upon my parents, to do good deeds that please You, and by Your mercy allow me to be considered amongst Your righteous servants."

The entire army looked in amazement. Despite having so much power, wealth, and a magnificent kingdom, Prophet Sulaiman was the humblest man in the world. In all my years, whenever I saw someone who had wealth and power, they would usually become arrogant and attribute their success to themselves. However, the wise person is the one who, when he succeeds, knows deep inside his heart that anything good that happens is a gift from Allah. Such a wise person then expresses his thanks to Allah. I learned this from watching Prophet Sulaiman and his father, Prophet Dawud. They preached and practiced gratitude all day and night.

After he finished making *dua*, he stopped to

take attendance of all the soldiers and members of his army. "*Jinn*, report your status!" After checking on all the *jinn*, he called out, "Foot soldiers, report your status!" After checking on the human soldiers, he was ready to address the birds. He turned his head towards the sky, and his blessed face was as bright as the full moon. As the radiant rays of the sun blinded his sight, he squinted his beautiful eyes and focused on the thousands of birds of nature soaring their way across the panorama. His eyebrows turned downward, and his face became red.

"How come I do not see the hud-hud? Is he amongst the absent?" he exclaimed in a loud, displeased tone. "I will surely punish him severely, perhaps even slaughter him, unless he gives me a good reason for his absence!"

A hushed murmur ran through the crowd. Members of the army began whispering amongst themselves.

"The hud-hud is one of the most reliable birds and is so trusted by Prophet Sulaiman. I wonder what made him disappear," said the first soldier.

"Yes, this is extraordinary," the second soldier responded. "He had better have a good excuse, or he will be in big trouble," he continued. The two soldiers went back and forth.

"Prophet Sulaiman loves the hud-hud. But he does not tolerate insubordination or misbehavior from any member of this army," warned the first soldier.

"The reason there is so much peace in his kingdom is because he makes sure the army is disciplined. If he was too relaxed with his soldiers, the kingdom's safety could be jeopardized," replied the second soldier.

"Yes, you are absolutely right. It's from the Prophet's love of his people and desire for safety that he must be so strict. Our job as soldiers is a matter of life and death for our people. If another tribe or nation perceives that our army is not disciplined, they might try to attack us. However, they know that Prophet Sulaiman is very vigilant and diligent, so they dare not try and attack us," said the first soldier.

"*Alhamdulillah*, we are so blessed by Allah to have a king who takes such good care of his kingdom," replied the second soldier.

It must have felt like hours had passed due to all the tension created because I was missing. But, it was just a few minutes until a little colorful speck was spotted in the horizon.

"Look, something is fluttering quickly towards us. That flight pattern is unmistakable. It's the hud-hud!" yelled a soldier.

Just like that, I landed in the valley right next to Prophet Sulaiman. And by the look on the Prophet's face, I knew I had some explaining to do.

A Letter to Saba

After catching my breath, I explained the cause of my absence.

"O Prophet Sulaiman, I have learned something that you are unaware of, for I have come from the land of Saba with astounding news."

Prophet Sulaiman listened attentively. He had no problem with a tiny bird like myself telling him that I knew something he did not. Being humble is a virtue of the righteous, and Prophet Sulaiman was the master of humble confidence.

"I have found a woman ruling over the people of Saba. She has been given everything that a ruler could desire, and she has a magnificent throne. But I have found her telling her people that the sun is their god. I have heard her commanding her people to worship the sun instead of Allah. *Shaytan* has deceived them into thinking that their deeds are good, and he has diverted them from the straight path, and thus they are misguided," I said.

"Sadly, they do not prostrate to Allah, the

One who brings forth what is hidden in the skies, the earth, and knows everything that you hide and what you declare," replied Prophet Sulaiman. "There is no god but Allah, and to Him belongs the most magnificent throne! We will indeed see if you are truthful or if you are lying," he warned.

The news I had just brought was serious. Prophet Sulaiman would consider this an international crisis that may warrant *jihad*, which meant a religious military intervention. The inhabitants of Saba did not have the freedom to worship Allah. The leaders controlled their citizens through propaganda and forced them to worship the sun. In such cases of religious oppression, *jihad* was a viable option.

Prophet Sulaiman had to make sure that everything I said was completely accurate. He would not act in haste without confirming the truth. But it didn't bother me that he had to confirm my report. This was his responsibility as the head of state, to make sure he didn't act on information unless he was sure of its authenticity. However, I think he believed me, because he did not seem to want to punish me. I had been a loyal servant for many years and had never lied to him before.

Prophet Sulaiman ordered the army to prepare itself. He decided that this international crisis in Saba was his top priority. The thought of people being forced to worship the sun made him incredibly uncomfortable. The inhabitants of every land must have the freedom to worship Allah if they desire. Forcing people to worship the sun was a great crime in the eyes of Prophet Sulaiman. Worshipping the creation instead of the Creator was the epitome of darkness and misguidance. He felt compelled to intervene. Once he returned to his palace, he called for his royal pen and paper and began to write a letter. He focused intensely on his writing and did not lift his head until he finished. He rolled up the paper and used his ring to stamp the letter, so the people of Saba knew it was an official document from his kingdom.

He securely fastened it and said to me, "Here, take this letter of mine and deliver it to the people of Saba. Then, wait and watch for what they decide to do."

I immediately took the letter in my claws and left for Saba. The journey would take some time, but I did not pace myself. I flew as fast as I could. I knew how much it pained Prophet Sulaiman to know that people were worshipping the sun instead of Allah, and he was keen on knowing how they would respond to his *dawah*.

After what felt like days, I arrived in Saba and went straight towards the palace of Queen Bilqis. It was a charming residence, but nothing compared to the grand palace of Prophet Sulaiman. The Queen's Guard consisted of countless soldiers protecting every entrance. I saw a beautiful arched window that was cracked open just an inch or two. I made a run towards the window and slipped in undetected. The Queen's Guard was built to stop a person or army. They did not suspect a tiny bird would try to sneak in.

I made my way around the palace looking for Queen Bilqis. Each time I saw a door open, I

snuck in quietly. The palace was designed intricate-
ly, and I had to sneak through seven doors until I
finally entered the room of Queen Bilqis. She was
reclining on her marvelous throne, which had giant,
gorgeous gemstones all around it. It was also draped
with the finest silk canopy. I noticed there was a
small hole in the canopy that had been carefully
made. When the sun would shine through the hole,
she would pray to the sun. I carefully flew towards
the throne and hovered right over the hole. I released the letter from my claws and it fell right onto
her lap. I then hid myself behind the throne and
listened.

"What is this?" wondered Queen Bilqis,
confused by the piece of parchment that had fallen
from the sky into her lap.

She immediately removed the string and
unrolled the letter. She saw the royal seal of King
Sulaiman and quickly read the letter. Then she came
down from her throne and called out, "My advisors,
please gather around. I have important news to tell
you. A noble letter was delivered to me. It has been

written on the finest paper I have ever seen. It has been written in the finest penmanship I have ever seen. It has the most elegant seal I have ever seen. It has come from none other than the great King Sulaiman."

"What does it say?" asked one of her advisors.

"Let me give you a gist of what the letter says," said Queen Bilqis.

"From King Sulaiman, the Prophet of Allah, to the honorable Queen Bilqis," the queen began reading. "I write this letter to you in the name of Allah, the most Merciful. I invite you to believe in Allah and accept our religion. Do not be arrogant in your beliefs. Rather, humbly come to me as Muslims, believing in Allah alone."

All the queen's advisors were silent, wondering where this letter came from and what it meant. The queen waited patiently for a response from her advisors, but after a few moments of hearing nothing but silence, she said, "O my advisors, tell me your opinions in this matter of mine. I never make

a decision unless you are in my presence."

The advisors took a moment and discussed with each other. Then, one man stepped forward and spoke on behalf of the group. "O your majesty, we are men of strength and military power," he said. "We do not have an opinion in diplomatic and political matters; the decision is yours alone. You decide what you think is best and give us orders."

Queen Bilqis thought for a moment and gathered her words. She replied to her advisors, "King Sulaiman is asking us to abandon our religion of sun worship. He believes the sun is merely a creation and is not worthy of worship. He believes that only Allah, who he claims is the Creator of the universe, including the sun, is worthy of worship. He threatens to invade our land to liberate our people to worship Allah if we don't listen to him. And whenever kings invade a city to conquer it, they destroy the city and humiliate the most honorable people in it."

The queen was incredibly wise. She knew well the history of the world, including the history of the region. She understood the behavior of kings and how kingdoms would expand and conquer foreign lands. So she devised an interesting plan to avoid war or any military conflict. She explained her plan to her advisors. "In response to his letter, I will send the king a gift instead of accepting or rejecting his offer. Then, we will see what response the messengers bring back."

It seemed her plan was to test Prophet Sulaiman with the lure of wealth. If he was only a king concerned with wealth, then Prophet Sulaiman might accept her generous gift and leave her and the land of Saba alone. After all, most kings of the world covet wealth and power, so if his concern was acquiring as much wealth as he could in this life, then he would be appeased by such a materialistic gift.

The Queen got off her throne and walked towards an elaborately carved wooden armoire in her room. She pulled out a beautiful handbag filled with gold. It was quite a generous gift from the queen. She handed the bag to one of her advisors, who then gave it to the royal envoy with instructions to deliver the gift immediately to the palace of King Sulaiman. I followed the ambassadors in the envoy all the way from the city of Marib in Saba to the land of Sham, where King Sulaiman's palace was located.

Not for Sale

The royal envoy finally arrived in Jerusalem after a long journey. They marveled at the Kingdom of Prophet Sulaiman, as they scanned the landscape in amazement.

"Look at the size of that!" said Rajul, a member of the envoy, as he pointed at a huge statue of a lion.

"Check out the gigantic cauldrons and reservoirs," he continued.

"Look at that palace! Have you ever seen anything more majestic? This is indubitably the greatest kingdom in the history of the world. Who and what could build such a magnificent kingdom?" said Safeer, who was the head ambassador of the envoy.

They continued walking along the path leading to the palace until they reached the royal court of Prophet Sulaiman. They were met by the guards at the entrance.

"We come to you from the land of Saba on

behalf of our leader, Queen Bilqis. She has received this letter from King Sulaiman, and we are here with her response. May we have the honor of meeting King Sulaiman and giving him a message and gift from the queen?" asked Safeer.

"Come in, please. King Sulaiman awaits you," answered the guard.

The royal envoy of Queen Bilqis entered and was immediately offered the finest food and drinks. It was the custom of Prophet Sulaiman and all prophets to honor their guests in this manner. After taking a moment to eat and quench their thirst, they were granted permission to enter the court and present Queen Bilqis' gift to Prophet Sulaiman. The ambassador, Safeer, walked towards Prophet Sulaiman, and said, "O honorable King Sulaiman. We come to you from the land of Saba, from the city of Marib. We come to you on behalf of our noble Queen Bilqis. She has received your letter and presents this gift to you as a token of her respect and awe for you and your glorious kingdom." He then handed the large handbag of gold to Prophet

Sulaiman.

Prophet Sulaiman took hold of the handbag and felt its contents. He opened the bag and peered inside, seeing hundreds upon hundreds of brilliant, gleaming gold coins. Prophet Sulaiman raised his gaze and gave a puzzled look to the royal envoy. Could they not see the majestic kingdom of Prophet Sulaiman? Did they not see his power and wealth on full display as soon as they entered the boundaries of the land of Sham? What good is a bag of gold to a king who has been granted far more wealth, power, and wisdom by Allah? Prophet Sulaiman looked upon the envoy with sympathy and frustration. He responded to them firmly.

"What is this? Do you wish to provide me with wealth? On the contrary, it is Allah who has given me far better than that which you bring me. It is not just wealth that He has given me, but knowledge, wisdom, and prophethood. Thus, I have no desire for such a gift. It is people like you who rejoice when receiving a valuable worldly gift."

What poor souls. They did not understand

that although Prophet Sulaiman had all the material luxury in the world, he was not motivated by money. Allah had given him all the wealth that one could desire, but Allah had also given him something far more valuable than money or power. Allah had granted Sulaiman prophethood, knowledge, and wisdom. These gifts allowed him to deeply understand the nature of this world, that it was temporary and not worth the wing of a mosquito compared to what Allah had prepared in the afterlife. Thus, his only motivation in life was to please Allah. Prophet Sulaiman was incredibly grateful for all the blessings he had been given by Allah, and he was constantly sharing his blessings with the citizens of his kingdom. He would never accept such a gift, because it was actually a bribe. It was an attempt to see if Prophet Sulaiman would sell his religion for wealth. It was a test of whether he would abandon inviting people to Allah for riches.

After giving the ambassador and his envoy a moment to reflect upon his response, Prophet Sulaiman continued.

"Go back to your people," he declared. "Let them know that if they do not allow their people to worship Allah freely, we will surely come to them with an unstoppable army. Then, we will drive them out of Saba in humiliation, and they will be absolutely belittled."

The envoy was in a state of shock. They were in awe of Prophet Sulaiman and began trembling in fear. They hastened back to Saba with Queen Bilqis' gift still in their hands. Faced with a long journey back home, it would take many days for the envoy to inform Queen Bilqis of Prophet Sulaiman's response to her gift. I kept a close eye on them as they left and overheard them speaking to one another about the events that had just transpired.

"This king is different. He does not care for money," said Rajul.

"Yes, I have never seen anyone like him," replied Safeer. "His presence is awe-inspiring. I was terrified upon seeing his disgust of the gift, yet greatly admired his composure and commitment to his religion."

"It's unbelievable. He doesn't want to attack our land for the natural resources we have, nor for the wealth that Queen Bilqis possesses. All he wants is for us to worship Allah!" Rajul exclaimed.

"I wonder what Queen Bilqis will think when she finds out what happened. It seems she doesn't want to fight King Sulaiman, and I can understand why. His army would destroy us in no time," replied Safeer.

"Yes, I agree. But she is a brilliant queen, she will figure something out," said Rajul.

I continued following the royal envoy all the way back to Saba.

Diplomacy

The royal envoy arrived in Saba and went straight to the queen's palace. The royal envoy entered through the seven doors to finally reach Queen Bilqis. She was seated on her magnificent throne, patiently waiting to hear about King Sulaiman's reaction to her gift. The ambassador, Safeer, asked for permission to speak, and after receiving her approval, he informed her of what had taken place with King Sulaiman.

"Dear honorable Queen Bilqis, we come to you with news from the holy city of Jerusalem," Safeer began. "The Kingdom of Sulaiman is like no other kingdom we have ever witnessed. His palace is like no other palace we have ever visited. King Sulaiman is like no other king we have encountered before. His kingdom is splendid in every way imaginable. He possesses wealth that one's mind cannot fathom. He possesses power that would make every king and queen jealous and completely dumbfounded. He possesses an impressive army comprised of powerful beasts, birds, and men that strikes fear into the hearts of their enemies.

We were received by the high council of *Bani Israil* with honor and dignity. King Sulaiman was most benevolent with us, offering us exquisite food and drinks upon our arrival. Then we presented the gift from your highness to King Sulaiman. Unfortunately, he did not receive the gift well. Rather, he considered it a bribe and rejected it completely. He informed us that Allah has given him far superior material wealth and that he has no need for our worldly gifts. He informed us that Allah has granted him knowledge, wisdom, and prophethood. He said that awareness of Allah is the ultimate gift. He then sent a warning that he will order his tremendous army straight to Saba if we do not submit to him and persist in worshipping the sun."

Queen Bilqis listened attentively, not interrupting her ambassador until he was finished speaking. I was impressed with her character. Her conduct was dignified in every way. After she heard the entire story, she thought for a moment and replied, "My people, this is a king like no other king we have ever encountered. He neither covets our land nor our wealth. His goal is not the mere expansion of his kingdom. Rather, his only desire is that we abandon worshipping the sun and believe in Allah. He believes the sun is nothing more than the creation of the One, true God."

Her advisors listened with great concern. I could sense their discomfort. They knew how to wage wars, but   diplomacy with a such a unique king was beyond their experience and knowledge. The queen continued speaking with her gentle, yet confident voice.

"Considering recent events, where the threat of invasion is real, we have two choices. On the one hand, we could gather all our forces and try to fight back against King Sulaiman and his army, but I believe this would be futile," Queen Bilqis reasoned. "His army is far more superior than our army in every imaginable way. He has birds, predators, humans, and even the *jinn* in his ranks. He has the most advanced technology of our times, including the most elaborate body armor known to mankind. I have even heard reports that he can control the wind and unleash it on his enemies. Thus, I believe that a second, wiser, option is to undertake another diplomatic mission. Since this man is not concerned with wealth or power, I must go myself and talk to him. Then, I will be able to determine if he is telling the truth about his religion and whether he is really a Prophet of Allah. I believe this is the only way to avoid a devastating attack on our land."

Her advisors hesitantly nodded in agreement. Once again, they were witnessing the wisdom of their queen. Queen Bilqis excused her advisors and immediately made preparations for her trip. She left instructions to her advisors concerning the affairs of Saba. She packed light and left with just a few members of the royal envoy to see for herself what this King Sulaiman was all about.

Wisdom in Judgment

I returned to Jerusalem the following morning. I found Prophet Sulaiman in the Royal Court, as this was his daily routine. Every morning, he would give his citizens an opportunity to consult him regarding any conflicts that they were having. The Royal Court was held in a large, regal building near his palace. It was an imposing structure that was built by the enslaved *jinn*.

Prophet Sulaiman was well known for his wisdom in legal judgments. He had demonstrated his intelligence and wisdom during the reign of his father, Prophet Dawud, which earned him the praise and respect of his people. Let me take a moment, if you please, to share with you a few of those stories.

One day, two women came to Prophet Dawud's court to dispute a very serious issue. The two women were not alone. They had a young infant with them. The infant was not old enough to walk or crawl. One of the women was young, and the other was a little older. They presented their cases before Prophet Dawud. The older woman introduced the issue.

"We have a serious problem for which we seek your help," she implored. "Both of us have recently been blessed with a baby. We were out in the city and we put our babies down for a moment to rest. Suddenly, a wolf came out of nowhere and snatched this woman's baby away."

The younger woman interrupted. "No, that is not true! The wolf took your baby. The living baby belongs to me."

The older woman quickly responded. "No, my dear, you are mistaken. I clearly saw your child being dragged away, and I quickly grabbed my child. Look, doesn't this baby look more like me?"

The two women argued back and forth, and Prophet Dawud heard both sides. In the end, after evaluating the limited evidence and testimony of the two women, he made a decision.

"It is my opinion, after hearing your testimonies, that the child should be given to you," Prophet

Dawud said, as he pointed to the older woman.

The older woman was delighted and took the baby. The younger woman was devastated and began crying, her tears pouring out of her eyes like raindrops falling from the sky. Prophet Sulaiman had walked in during the middle of the case and heard the verdict. All of a sudden, he called out to the royal staff in the court.

"Please, someone go and grab me a knife."

Everyone was puzzled. Why would he ask for a knife? There was no food around and a serious child custody case had just concluded. Nonetheless, without saying a word, one of the royal staff immediately obeyed the command of the Prophet and brought him a sharp knife. Prophet Sulaiman grabbed the knife and proclaimed, "Since the evidence in the case was not so clear and conclusive to grant one woman the child over the other, I think it is fair that instead we cut the baby in half and give each woman half a child."

The two women listened and had very different responses. The older woman stood there, quiet and stoic, showing no emotion after hearing Prophet Sulaiman's suggestion. However, the younger woman had the opposite reaction.

"No! No! Please don't. May Allah have mercy on you. Let her keep the baby. The baby can be hers. Just don't hurt the baby. I beg you," she pled.

Prophet Sulaiman looked at the older woman. "You did not seem concerned when I suggested cutting the child in half. Why is that?"

The older woman replied, "Uh, uh, uh..." Then, she began to cry and said in a subdued tone, "To be honest, I wasn't completely truthful in my testimony. I really wanted this child because something terrible happened to my own child. The truth of the matter is that the wolf ate my child, and that is why I wanted this baby to replace the child I lost. But this baby actually belongs to her."

Prophet Sulaiman took the baby and gave it to the younger woman. What wisdom he had! He was quickly able to determine that the younger woman was the real mother of the child, because she became distressed upon hearing the baby would be cut in half. This was a clear indication that the baby belonged to her, for she loved the baby so much that she would rather give up the baby than have the baby cut in half or harmed in any way. No mother could fathom her child being cut into two pieces.

On another occasion, two men came to the court of Prophet Dawud. They explained that they had a case concerning property destruction that they needed to resolve. Prophet Dawud asked the plaintiff, a farmer, to present his case.

"Good morning, Prophet Dawud," the farmer began. "This man is my neighbor. He is a good man. However, he has been quite negligent with his sheep. The other day, he left his entire herd of sheep alone and they wandered onto my farmland and destroyed all my crops. The entire season's harvest! These crops were very valuable! What am I to do for this season, now that I have been left with nothing? How can I expect to support myself and my family? I am seeking compensation for the damages to my crops and farmland."

The neighbor, a shepherd, responded, "It is true that my sheep destroyed his crops. But it was an accident! The sheep escaped from their pen at night, perhaps due to the lock not being secured. When I woke up in the morning and saw my sheep were no longer in their pen, I quickly gathered them from my neighbor's farmland, but it was too late! The damage had been done," the shepherd lamented. "I am so sorry for the huge loss it has caused my neighbor. And while I would like to compensate him, I do not possess the wealth to repay him in full."

Prophet Dawud deliberated for a moment. Prophet Sulaiman was listening quietly, assiduously studying the details of the case. He was just a young man back then, perhaps in his early teens. Prophet Dawud gave his judgment.

"I understand that no malice was intended. It was indeed an accident. Nonetheless, the owner of the sheep is liable due to his negligence, as he did not properly secure the pen and look after his sheep. The farmer has done no wrong. Since you possess no additional wealth to compensate the farmer with, I award the farmer all of your sheep as restitution."

Just then, Prophet Sulaiman approached his father and whispered to him. "Father, may I have a word with you?"

"Of course, my son," Prophet Dawud replied.

"While your ruling is reasonable and fair, I have a suggestion that may work better for both parties. The farmer would ideally like his farmland and harvest restored, and the shepherd does not want to lose his sheep. Why don't the shepherd and farmer swap their assets temporarily? This way, the farmer can benefit from the milk, wool, and offspring of the sheep, while the shepherd can take care of the farmland. Once the farmland has been restored to its previous condition, then each party can take back their original assets.

Prophet Dawud agreed this was a better resolution. Prophet Dawud gave the farmer and shepherd the new verdict. Both were happy with the judgment and thanked the Prophets for resolving the case. *SubhanAllah*! Prophet Sulaiman was a genius. Now you can see why his court was very busy every day. *Bani Israil* was confident that their prophet would solve their problems with wisdom and fairness.

These are just a few stories about Prophet Sulaiman's incredible wisdom. I could spend hours narrating more of them to you, but perhaps for another day. I just wanted you to appreciate his wisdom with these few anecdotes. May Allah bless his soul and allow us to learn from his perfect example. Now let me get back to telling you about my return from Saba with the news of Queen Bilqis' arrival.

Test of Thrones

I rushed into the Royal Court and immediately informed Prophet Sulaiman that Queen Bilqis was on her way from Saba to visit him. I mentioned that she would be arriving soon, probably later today.

The Prophet was impressed with her decision to avoid conflict. He realized that her choice to meet with him was the perfect opportunity to explain the religion of Islam to her and prove his prophethood. If Queen Bilqis believed in Sulaiman's prophethood, then she would accept Islam. If she accepted Islam, perhaps the people of Saba would become Muslims. This, after all, was the Prophet's goal. He wanted people to be guided to Allah. If they became Muslims, they would attain Allah's pleasure and benefit in this life and in the afterlife from their obedience to Allah.

Queen Bilqis was only a few hours away from arriving in Jerusalem when Prophet Sulaiman summoned his royal council for an emergency meeting.

"O royal councilmen, I have an important announcement," he said. "Bilqis, the Queen of Saba, is on her way to meet me. Before she comes, I have a request. Which of you can bring me her throne before she and her people come to me in submission?"

One of the powerful *jinn* from his council spoke. "I will bring it to you before you complete your court judgments for today. For this task, I am strong and trustworthy."

Prophet Sulaiman was impressed with the *jinn's* confidence. Court would still be in session until noon, so the *jinn* was claiming he could travel from Jerusalem to Saba and back within a few short hours.

"Thank you for your offer," replied Prophet Sulaiman. "Can anyone bring it to me faster than this powerful *jinn*?" he asked.

Another member of the council named Asif spoke up. Asif was known to have incredible knowledge of scripture.

"I will bring it to you before you can even blink," he offered.

Sure enough, before Prophet Sulaiman could blink, he saw the magnificent throne of Queen Bilqis before him. He stood silent for a moment, in deep reflection, and said, "This is from the abundant favors that my Lord has given me. All of the favors that I have been given are tests from Allah. He wants to see whether I am grateful or ungrateful to Him."

Everyone around him listened quietly, soaking up his wisdom and insight. He elaborated further, "Whoever is grateful to Allah will personally benefit from their gratitude. Whoever is ungrateful, then you must know that my Lord is the most wealthy and powerful. He does not need anyone's gratitude. He is the most generous."

It was a common occurrence to hear Prophet Sulaiman speak about gratitude, for gratitude was one of the keys to wisdom. Grateful people are happy and satisfied with what Allah has given them. Grateful people do not become jealous when others are blessed. Gratitude humbles and removes arrogance. Gratitude propels us to share our blessings with others. At that moment, I felt so grateful to be a humble servant to Prophet Sulaiman.

None of us understood exactly why Prophet Sulaiman requested her throne, because he did not explain his reasons to us. However, many of the people of knowledge around me have spoken about his motives. I will share with you some of what they said. First, Prophet Sulaiman wanted to prove his prophethood to her. If he could have her throne brought to him before her arrival, she would understand that this was a miracle from Allah. How else could he retrieve her throne, which was locked in her palace behind seven doors, without bringing an army to march in and take it by force?

Second, she would realize the miraculous power that Allah had granted Prophet Sulaiman, including his ability to control the *jinn*. This would make her more inclined to believe in his prophethood and his message.

Finally, it would be a confirmation of my

initial reports. If you remember, I had earlier told him about her throne and how splendidly it was decorated and how elaborate the craftsmanship was. Prophet Sulaiman wanted to see if my description was accurate.

As for the details of how the throne was brought from Saba to Jerusalem in a matter of seconds, I wish I could tell you. However, I was not privy to such secrets. The only thing I can tell you is that knowledge is more powerful than physical strength. The *jinn* was much stronger physically than the one with knowledge, yet he could not bring the throne to Prophet Sulaiman as fast as the one with knowledge.

Prophet Sulaiman now commanded his council. "Disguise her throne for her. We will see whether she will be guided to the truth of the matter or if she will be from the people who are not guided."

Now we understood the wisdom behind Prophet Sulaiman bringing her throne to Jerusalem. It would be used as an intelligence test. Would she be intelligent enough to recognize her throne, or would she be clueless? We would soon find out.

The Queen's Decision

Prophet Sulaiman's workers began diligently refashioning the queen's throne. One of the hallmarks of her throne was the elaborate embedding of rare gemstones all around it. They removed the brilliant green emeralds and replaced them with glimmering purple garnets. They swapped the exquisite blue sapphire with radiant red rubies. They exchanged the sparkling diamonds with rare fire opal. Then they redecorated the seat and arms of the throne with a different pattern of silk tapestry. The altered throne looked even more majestic than the original. Prophet Sulaiman was satisfied with the transformation and placed the throne outside of his palace. He waited patiently for the queen's arrival.

Queen Bilqis arrived a short time after and was greeted by the royal council. She introduced herself.

"I am Bilqis, Queen of Saba, and I have come to meet with the honorable King Sulaiman."

"Welcome. Welcome. He has been expecting you," replied the head councilman. "Please proceed towards the palace. He will meet you outside in the terrace. Feel free to have a look around and enjoy yourself."

As she walked towards the palace, she was flabbergasted by the marvelous kingdom before her. She looked all around her, awestruck by the imposing fortresses and enormous water reservoirs. The queen whispered under her breath, "The architecture of each building is exquisite. There is no way that humans could have built all of this.

Each structure is so unique and fits in perfectly with the design of the city. The buildings have elaborate brick designs, vaulted ceilings, and gorgeous shingles. They have huge arches and domes. The fortresses are vast, with tall stone turrets and battlements. What creature could create such colossal fortresses, cauldrons, and reservoirs?" She continued to scan the vicinity in wonder. She moved her head slowly to the left, then to the right, until she became fixated on the spring of copper nearby.

"A natural spring of flowing metal? That's not possible," she said to herself incredulously.

Queen Bilqis continued walking slowly into the terrace and saw a dignified looking man waiting for her.

"That must be King Sulaiman. He looks very distinguished and proper," she said to herself.

Queen Bilqis approached Prophet Sulaiman hesitantly. She was known to be a woman of composure with nerves of steel, yet at that moment she found herself quite nervous. Her heart was up to her throat and her legs were shaking like saplings in the wind. The presence of Prophet Sulaiman intimidated her.

Prophet Sulaiman greeted her graciously, "Welcome, Bilqis, honorable Queen of Saba. We have been waiting for your arrival. I have something to show you."

"I wonder what he wants to show me," she pondered.

Beside Prophet Sulaiman was the queen's throne, concealed under a large cloth. A member of the royal council pulled the cloth off the throne to reveal to Queen Bilqis the brilliant item that lay underneath it.

"Do you have a throne like this?" asked Prophet Sulaiman.

Queen Bilqis gazed upon the throne, scrutinizing it closely. She curiously walked around the throne, noticing the new silk tapestry and different gemstones all around it. However, the structure of the throne was the exact same as her own throne. She was perplexed.

She thought to herself, "How could Sulaiman have such a similar throne? There is no way my throne can be here in Jerusalem. I am positive I left it behind in my palace in Saba. It is incredibly heavy and well-guarded. But this man has shown me he is no ordinary man…He has amazing superpowers. Perhaps he really is a prophet sent by Allah!"

She thought for a moment about how to craft her response most intelligently. "It is as though it was," she replied.

What a response! She neither said it was

her exact throne nor that it was not like her throne. She passed Sulaiman's intelligence test and he was indeed impressed with her response. He cracked a smile.

As Prophet Sulaiman's royal council observed her response and his satisfaction with her intelligence, they spoke amongst themselves.

"It seems as if she is beginning to realize the miraculous powers that Allah has given Prophet Sulaiman," one councilman said. "However, we have been given knowledge of his miracles well before her. And we have already submitted to Allah. Her worship of the sun has prevented her from understanding the truth. Indeed, she has come from a disbelieving people."

Prophet Sulaiman then proceeded to the next part of the queen's visit. He led her toward the doors of the palace. The doors were made of solid wood and had intricate carvings on them. They were flawless. The doors were at least ten feet tall and six inches thick.

"Please, enter the palace," said Prophet

Sulaiman, gesturing towards the entrance.

The double doors opened inward. She took a step forward. Just as her left leg was about to come down, her eyes caught sight of the floor beneath her. She saw nothing but crystal-clear water beneath her. There was coral in the water and various species of the most beautiful fish in the world. The fish were different colors, shapes, and sizes. Bright orange, yellow, white, red, purple, and more. Some were long, and some were short. Some were fat, and some were skinny. There were all kinds of sea creatures swimming around. Just as she felt she was about to fall into the water, she pulled up her long dress to keep it from getting soaked. This caused her ankles to be exposed. However, to her amazement, her foot landed onto the solid floor and she stumbled for a moment before regaining her footing.

"What is going on? Is this for real?" she wondered in awe.

Prophet Sulaiman followed behind her and entered the palace. He saw the look of amazement

on Queen Bilqis' face. He turned towards her and informed her of what she was walking on.

"Indeed, this is a palace made of perfectly smooth quartz glass floors," said Prophet Sulaiman.

Queen Bilqis was speechless, but a million thoughts were running through her mind.

"No man can create such a kingdom. Everything I am witnessing is a miracle from Allah. This palace is a miracle from Allah! The aquarium beneath my feet is a miracle from Allah! My throne being brought here from Saba is a miracle from Allah! The buildings and architecture are miracles from Allah. The ability to communicate with the animals is a miracle from Allah. The power to control the *jinn* is a miracle from Allah. The spring of liquid copper is a miracle from Allah. The power to control the wind is a miracle from Allah. It is only the One, true God that has given these miracles and superpowers to this humble servant of His. Allah has indeed given the treasures of this life to Sulaiman. He has been given gratitude, knowledge, wisdom, and prophethood.

I have been deceived by my reliance on my eyes and senses. I have always believed that nothing is true unless I can see it or sense it. How foolish I was! I saw the water before my eyes and believed I would fall into it, but there was a quartz glass floor on top of it. I saw the huge sun shining bright in the sky and believed it was our creator. How foolish I was! The veil has been lifted from my eyes and now my heart sees the truth. Human perception is limited, but the knowledge of Allah is perfect. The *ghayb* is real, and it is only known to Allah."

She continued walking across the quartz crystal floors, admiring the perfection of the palace from above and below. Then, she turned towards Prophet Sulaiman and proclaimed to all in attendance, "My Lord, I have wronged myself for far too long. As of this moment, I happily submit to you, Allah, just as Prophet Sulaiman has. You are indeed the Lord of the worlds."

With those sincere words, Queen Bilqis entered the into the religion of Islam, the religion of Prophet Sulaiman and all the prophets of Allah.

Everyone in attendance was silent, but you could see the joy on their faces. This queen, who had spent her entire life ignorantly worshipping the sun, was now fully aware of her true purpose in life. She understood that belief in Allah and obedience to His Prophet was the key to happiness and paradise.

Just then, I realized I had to fly off to tend to my other responsibilities. I was not there to witness what happened next, nor was it my concern. I was taught that what matters is that the truth be conveyed, and I was a witness that it had been. I heard from the others that Queen Bilqis left the palace shortly after to return to Saba and invite her people to believe in Allah, following the way of Prophet Sulaiman.

One Last Matter

Prophet Sulaiman felt a great sense of gratitude. His royal council was incredibly pleased with the outcome. They spoke excitedly amongst themselves.

"*Alhamdulillah*, what an immense blessing from Allah!" exclaimed a councilman.

"Absolutely. Prophet Sulaiman has guided another person to the truth, to believe in Allah and to follow His prophets. That is indeed the key to success in this life and in the afterlife," replied a sage.

"We might have sent an army to Saba, but the intelligence of Queen Bilqis saved her people," said the councilman.

"Most certainly. True intelligence is to believe in Allah. True intelligence is to follow His Prophets and Messengers. Despite all the manifest signs of Allah's existence, there are still people who believe in all kinds of foolishness," replied the sage.

"*SubhanAllah*! The creation of the

heavenly bodies is a sign of Allah. The creation of the animals is a sign of Allah. The creation of man is a sign of Allah," the sage continued.

"If only *Bani Israil* wouldn't be so stubborn. While some of them believe in Islam, the religion of Prophet Sulaiman, there are many who still believe in the power of the *jinn* and the power of magic," said the councilman.

"Astounding. Prophet Sulaiman was able to guide a sun-worshipping queen to Allah, yet some of *Bani Israil* still disbelieve and spread corruption," continued the councilman shaking his head. "Don't worry. The truth will always triumph. Allah has a way of teaching people a lesson," said the sage, assuring the councilman.

As time passed, news spread about the miracles of Prophet Sulaiman. Many tribes and people heard about his kingdom and his religion. They heard about his humility and gratitude. They learned how to appreciate Allah's blessings. They heard about his wisdom, and they were mesmerized by stories of his ingenious solutions to people's dilemmas.

However, the *jinn* and their evil followers were a constant scourge in Prophet Sulaiman's kingdom. They kept spreading lies that the *jinn* knew the *ghayb* and had more power than our great king and prophet. Prophet Sulaiman's closest advisors kept a close eye on these troublemakers and discussed how to deal with the matter amongst themselves.

"These evil *jinn* worshippers keep spreading falsehoods. They are telling the people that the *jinn* know the *ghayb*. They are telling the people that Prophet Sulaiman is merely a magician! They are polluting the minds of innocent people with all kinds of filth! How can they say such preposterous things about our esteemed Prophet? What shall we do?" asked one advisor, visibly upset by the lies being spread.

"Perhaps we should punish them. We can put them in jail!" exclaimed another advisor.

At that moment, one of the wisest advisors chimed in. "Have patience, my dear brothers.

The criminals plot against Allah, but Allah will humiliate them when He wills and how He wills. Our job is to keep the peace and keep guiding people to the truth. Prophet Sulaiman knows best when to intervene."

Prophet Sulaiman deliberated over the matter for quite some time. He prayed to Allah to expose the liars and show the people that the *jinn* had no knowledge of the *ghayb*.

As time passed, our prophet aged graciously. One day, the angel of death approached him. In case you don't know, let me tell you something about the angel of death. He is a special angel who comes to take a person's soul when Allah commands him to. We were taught by our Prophet that the angel of death gently takes the soul of the believers like water flowing out of a bottle. However, when he is sent to a disbeliever, the angel rips his soul out painfully, like a comb being pulled through tangled hair. May Allah command the angel of death to remove our souls gently. Say *Aameen*!

When the angel of death approached

Prophet Sulaiman, he realized it was his time to leave this world. However, he had one last request. He put his hands up in *dua* and begged Allah, "Oh Allah, when you take my soul, hide my death from the evil *jinn*." Even in his death, Prophet Sulaiman wanted the people to learn a lesson.

He entered his prayer niche, a special room in his palace where he spent much of his time worshipping Allah. He would stand in prayer for so long that he had to lean on his cane to keep from falling from fatigue. He might even spend days or weeks in the room, worshipping Allah in seclusion. On this fateful day, he raised his hands and began to pray. Prophet Sulaiman focused intensely and recited the scripture quietly. No one was allowed to enter the room when he prayed, and there was no window to look into. However, there was a tiny hole in the door where you could peek in and see what the prophet was doing. As his prayer continued for many hours into the night, Prophet Sulaiman grabbed his cane and leaned on it.

One whole day passed, and he was still in

the room. Then, a second day passed. And a third. And on and on, for countless days and nights, Prophet Sulaiman was standing in his prayer niche and leaning on his cane in prayer. The people and the *jinn* began to wonder what was going on. Nonetheless, the *jinn* continued to work as they had been commanded by Prophet Sulaiman.

Meanwhile, Prophet Sulaiman continued standing. His body was bent slightly forward, with his right hand putting his body weight on the cane. The weight of his strong, muscular body made the cane creak. Slowly, it began to crack.

Suddenly, the most unimaginable thing happened. The entire cane snapped in half and there was a loud thud. There, on the floor of the most grand palace in the history of the world, lay the most magnificent man I have ever seen with my little bird eyes. Prophet Sulaiman had died. It was the saddest day of my life. I would have sacrificed anything in this world for his sake.

No one had spoken to the Prophet in quite some time. Therefore, we had no idea when he actually died. It could have been days or weeks. Only Allah knows the truth of the matter. Allah had ordered his soul to be taken while His prophet was in prayer and leaning on his cane. Therefore, he did not fall immediately when he died. He stood there for a long time, even though his heart had stopped beating long ago.

Allah had answered the prayer of Prophet Sulaiman. Remember, he had asked Allah to hide his death from the *jinn*. Therefore, the evil *jinn* had kept working because they thought he was alive the whole time. Word got out to *Bani Israil* and the citizens of the kingdom that Prophet Sulaiman had died some time ago.

Everyone was talking about it. I overheard one conversation between a man and woman from *Bani Israil*.

"Can you believe how King Sulaiman died?" said the man, incredulously.

"It's extraordinary. He died in prayer in his palace, and no one realized it for so long!" replied the woman.

"Yes. It is mind-boggling. No one in his palace noticed. No one in his family noticed. Not even the evil *jinn* who convinced us they knew the *ghayb* had noticed," replied the man.

"I feel like such a fool for believing the sorcerers and *jinn*. Our faith in them was misguided. What do we do now?" asked the woman.

"It's never to late to accept the truth. We have to admit that King Sulaiman was right. He warned us that the sorcerers were swindlers and frauds. He told us that they would use all sorts of trickery and lies from the *jinn* to deceive people. The enslaved *jinn* worked day and night for King Sulaiman, even though he was already dead. Had they actually known he was dead, they would have quit working," replied the man.

"I ask Allah to forgive me. From now on, I will put my trust in Allah and follow the scripture and guidance of our deceased Prophet," said the woman, resolutely.

"Me too," replied the man, his voice now subdued with humility after realizing his mistakes.

Indeed, the people realized that the *jinn* did not know the *ghayb*, because if they had known the unseen, they would have known that Prophet Sulaiman had died and they would have stopped working. It was only because his cane snapped that we became aware of his death. What made his cane snap after all those days and weeks? My friend, know that Allah has soldiers that no one else can see. They do what they are commanded in the most mysterious ways.

You see, as Prophet Sulaiman stood in prayer while leaning on his cane, a little termite crawled across the room and smelled the wooden cane. The termite slithered to the bottom of the cane and crawled to the middle of it. It took a tiny, termite-sized nibble out of the cane. The cane must have had the most exquisite smell, since the Prophet's blessed hands had been on it for quite some time. Anything that his blessed hands touched had the most pleasant aroma. The tiny termite, that no one saw or heard, kept nibbling away. It must have taken many days, but eventually the termite ate through a large piece of the cane, making it weak and creaky. Amazingly, Allah just had to send a tiny termite to remind the misguided people that only He knew the *ghayb*.

The people learned an important lesson with the death of our beloved Prophet. They learned that only Allah knows the *ghayb*. But, sadly, nothing would ever be the same again in our glorious kingdom. All the miracles that were given to our Prophet came to an abrupt end. The *jinn* were now free, so they ran away and stopped working. The wind was no longer something that could be controlled for our benefit. The spring of liquid copper dried up and stopped flowing. No one could understand the animals anymore. I was no longer an important soldier in the army. I was just another bird living in the beautiful land of Palestine.

I spent the rest of my life in worship. I would wake up early in the morning before sunrise and sing the praises of Allah outside of Masjid al-Aqsa. I would then leave my nest looking for worms and other insects to eat. I had complete trust in Allah

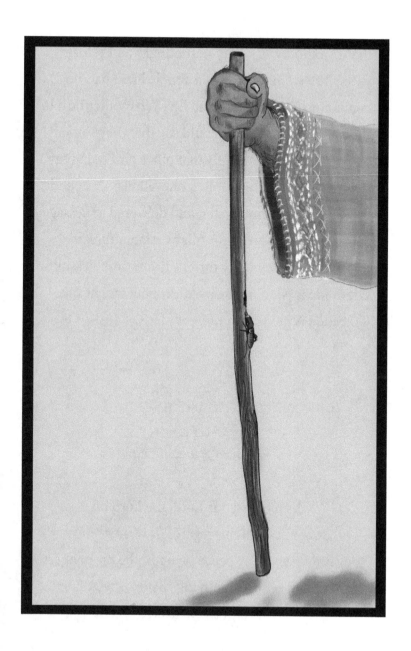

that I would fly from my nest hungry and return with a full stomach. It was a simple life. I had no complaints. I had lived a full life. What other bird in the history of the world could say that they served a Prophet the way I did? What other bird could say that they spoke to a prophet, obeyed his commands, helped his army find water, and delivered a message calling people to worship Allah? *Alhamdulillah*. I thank Allah immensely for His favors and blessings. Gratitude is what my beloved Prophet taught me. Gratitude is my way of life.

سُبْحَانَ رَبِّكَ رَبِّ الْعِزَّةِ عَمَّا يَصِفُونَ
وَسَلَامٌ عَلَى الْمُرْسَلِينَ
وَالْحَمْدُ لِلَّهِ رَبِّ الْعَالَمِينَ

Glorified is your Lord, the Lord of
Honor and Might, regardless of anything
they might say. May peace be upon the messengers.
Surely, all praise and thanks belongs to Allah,
Lord of the Universe.

The End

Author's Note

The stories of the prophets are the best of stories. They are not fairytales nor mere bedtime stories. They are real stories full of wisdom and lessons for mankind. From an Islamic perspective, one of the challenges of narrating these stories is ensuring that the information presented is accurate. As with any human endeavor to interpret the Islamic sources (Quran and hadith), there will be many opinions on the exact nature of the events that occurred. Therefore, I believe it important to explain the methodology of this series in presenting the lives of the prophets.

First, I have tried to avoid Israiliyaat, which refers to information transmitted from Jewish and Christian sources, to the best of my ability. However, there may be minor details about an event from these sources that I have incorporated, on the condition that they do not influence the theological or legal interpretation of an event.

Second, I have extensively researched classical and modern Islamic sources (e.g., tafsir, hadith, and history books) and have selected what I believe to be the most acceptable interpretation of events.

An acceptable interpretation is one that is considered authentic by Muslim scholarship or is in accordance with the spirit and principles of Islam. Therefore, the storyline may diverge from popular interpretations that I consider to be unreliable or difficult to reconcile with Islamic principles.

Third, I have included conversations that likely took place amongst some of the secondary characters in the story. I believe it is reasonable to infer some of the minor conversations that are not explicitly mentioned in the sources. I take comfort in knowing that this has been done by righteous scholars before me. For example, the great scholar of Islam, Abul Hasan Ali Nadwi, inferred many conversations in his famous Arabic book for children, Qasas al-Nabiyyeen (Stories of the Prophets). I have also made up the names of some of the minor secondary characters to improve the narrative flow of the novel.

I ask Allah to forgive me for any mistakes I have made, for indeed perfection is reserved for Allah and His prophets.

The Chronicles of Bani Israil will continue with more stories of the magnificent prophets…

About the Author

Dr. Osman Umarji is a scholar of Islam and educational psychology. He studied at Al-Azhar University in Cairo, Egypt, and received his Ph.D. in Education from the University of California, Irvine. He is currently the Director of Survey Research and Evaluation at the Yaqeen Institute For Islamic Research. He loves being out in nature amongst the trees, mountains, and birds with his wife and children in Southern California.

CPSIA information can be obtained
at www.ICGtesting.com
Printed in the USA
LVHW082052220121
676966LV00006BA/326

9 781733 826754